FRIENDS
OF ACPL

DO NOT REMOVE
CARDS FROM POCKET

1/89

THE PHANTOM
OF THE OPERETTA

OTHER MYSTERIES BY THE AUTHOR

Determined Detectives

Merger on the Orient Expressway

The Mysterious Case Case

Sebastian (Super Sleuth) and the
Bone to Pick Mystery

Sebastian (Super Sleuth) and the
Clumsy Cowboy

Sebastian (Super Sleuth) and the
Crummy Yummies Caper

Sebastian (Super Sleuth) and the
Hair of the Dog Mystery

Sebastian (Super Sleuth) and the
Purloined Sirloin

Sebastian (Super Sleuth) and the
Santa Claus Caper

Sebastian (Super Sleuth) and the
Secret of the Skewered Skier

DETERMINED DETECTIVES

THE PHANTOM
OF THE OPERETTA

by Mary Blount Christian

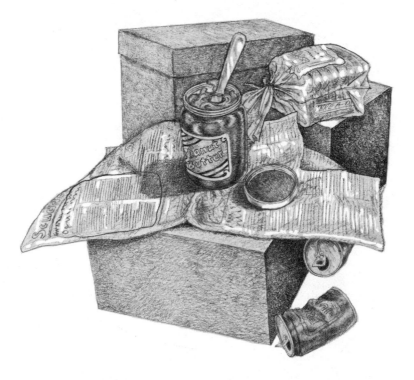

illustrated by Kathleen Collins Howell

E. P. DUTTON   NEW YORK

Text copyright © 1986 by Mary Blount Christian
Illustrations copyright © 1986 by Kathleen Collins Howell

Library of Congress Cataloging in Publication Data

Christian, Mary Blount.
    The phantom of the operetta.

(Determined Detectives)
    Summary: Intrepid detectives Fenton and Gerald and
their rival Mae Donna try to discover who or what is
haunting the local civic theater.
    [1. Mystery and detective stories]   I. Howell,
Kathleen Collins, ill.   II. Title.   III. Series:
Christian, Mary Blount.   Determined Detectives.
PZ7.C4528Ph   1986   [Fic]   86-11497
ISBN 0-525-44272-3

Published in the United States by E. P. Dutton,
2 Park Avenue, New York, N.Y. 10016

Published simultaneously in Canada by
Fitzhenry & Whiteside Limited, Toronto

Editor: Julie Amper

Printed in the U.S.A.   W   First Edition
10 9 8 7 6 5 4 3 2 1

7109742

remembering Dr. Laura C. Bickel,
a guardian angel for children

7109742

CONTENTS

What Could Be Worse?

School had closed for the summer. I'd read everything in the small public library—twice. The Scudder City Swimming Pool wasn't scheduled to open for a few weeks. What's worse, there hadn't been a mystery to solve in a month. And I, Fenton P. Smith, the more clever half of the Determined Detectives, felt at loose ends.

Gerald Grubbs, my *junior* partner, hadn't been to my house all week. Out-of-town company, he said. Who but Gerald counts *aunts* as company?

"Do something today, Fenton, something—constructive," Mom said. She was on her way to work, and I noticed she had one of those dumb women's magazines that is always giving readers tests. You know the kind: "Is Your Child an Achiever?" "Will Your Marriage Survive?" "Do Your Child's Manners Withstand the Torture Test?" Mom always takes those tests, and we never come out too good in them. Who would? Then she starts working on us to bring her score up. It's awful.

1

I had glanced at this month's test last night just to prepare myself. It's called "Is Your Child Headed for Trouble?" It asked things like Does your child sit around idly staring into space?

"Must you just sit there staring idly into space?" Mom asked as she crawled into her little car and slammed the door.

"I'm thinking, Mom!" I said. "Thinking is constructive."

She nodded happily, then blew me a kiss before she drove off. I settled back on the front steps of my house, my chin resting on my knees. I watched the lawn sprinkler spread a thin layer of water over the grass. Back and forth. Back and forth. Talk about boring!

I shifted my weight and sighed. "I am so bored, even Mae Donna Dockstadter would seem exciting about now." I spoke out loud, although I was the only one there. I was *so* bored that I was even talking to *myself*. I thought a minute about seeing Mae Donna. She's this dumb old girl from school. The only *good* thing about Mae Donna is her *father*; he's a secret agent. She told us so. You'd never guess from looking at him. He disguises himself as a pest exterminator. He probably wasn't counting on that blabbermouth daughter of his to spill the beans to me and Gerald. But he should know that he could count on *us* to keep his secret. We *professionals* have to stick together.

"Naw," I amended. "I don't want to see Mae Donna. I am not *that* desperate." Now I was so bored I was even *answering* myself.

I went inside and brought out the Scudder newspaper. Maybe there would be a story in there about something we could investigate. I thumbed through the newspaper, scanning the headlines: SWIMMING POOL OPENING DELAYED FOR REPAIRS. COMMUNITY THEATER OPENING IN OLD DRUMMOND MANSION, REPORTS TOWN HISTORIAN SAMANTHA TWILL. SCUDDER BULLDOGS SCORE ZIP IN GAME. Lots of other dull stuff, too. But something caught my eye. Some guy named Perciphal "Sticky Fingers" Potts had been released from prison last week.

That had possibilities. I read further. It said that Sticky Fingers had served his full sentence for robbery.

"I won't return to Scudder, man," Sticky Fingers said. "No way!" the article quoted. I could feel my heart quicken. The man had robbed. Why wouldn't he lie? Maybe he'd come back to Scudder and try to rob something else. The Determined Detectives could track him down. I read further. It said that the money—a million dollars—was taken from the Scudder National Bank, and it was never recovered. He had served his whole term without ever telling the police where he had hidden the money.

The guy was not only sticky fingered, but coolheaded. Just the kind of challenge we liked. Surely he would return to Scudder. Maybe we could tail him to where he had hidden the money. There was probably even a big reward for finding it.

First of all, we'd need to know what our quarry looked like. I had an idea. The Scudder newspaper probably covered the robbery when it happened. Maybe I could get a picture of him from an old newspaper

3

clipping. "Fenton P. Smith, you are a genius," I said aloud. I didn't bother to answer this time, but there was certainly no disagreement there.

I decided to stop off at the newspaper on my way to Gerald's house. But they might not let me into the newspaper building if they recognized me. Last time I was there, I accidentally backed into the button that starts the paper rolling through the presses. Poor Mr. Saxet, the publisher, was leaning over to do some last-minute proofreading and got his tie caught in the presses.

But did he remember that it was I who stopped the presses and saved him? No, all he remembers is that I started the whole mess in the first place. Now there is a sign on the door. It says, No Salesmen Allowed. No Fenton P. Smith, Either. I went to my room and rummaged through my toy box for a disguise. I put on a dirty trench coat and a false nose with an attached moustache. But just to play safe, I pulled a brown felt hat low over my face. Hastily I wrote *Press* on a piece of paper and stuck it in my hatband.

I took a notepad and an old instant camera. I might as well look like a reporter, I figured. The newspaper office was on Main, about five blocks north of Gerald's house.

I parked my bike outside the one-story building and went inside. I sidled over to the file cabinets where they stored old news clippings. I looked under *R* for *Robbery* and *P* for *Potts*. Nothing. Finally, I found the clipping under *S* for *Still in Prison*. That filing system made me wonder if dumb old Mae Donna Dockstadter had been working here.

Sure enough, the original story included a picture. Of course, it was fifteen years old and sort of faded. It would be hard to recognize Sticky Fingers from the old picture. I did notice that he had ears like a ship's sails, though. How many men look like the S.S. *Cuttysark*? That should make the job a little easier.

I scanned the story briefly and figured it was worth keeping. I quickly photocopied the story and picture, figuring I could read it more carefully later. I stuffed it in the back pocket of my jeans and hurried to leave the office before Mr. Saxet could spot me. I grabbed the door and yanked it open.

Unfortunately, Mr. Saxet was on the other side of the doorknob and tumbled in headfirst. I quickly helped him up, then made a flying leap out the door.

"The face isn't familiar," Mr. Saxet yelled, "but the modus operandi is. Is that you, Fenton P. Smith?"

I pedaled to Gerald's. I was just about to ring his doorbell when I heard something that was scary enough to curl my false moustache.

It was an absolutely blood-curdling scream, and it came from inside Gerald's house.

So Now We Know

"Don't worry, Gerald! I'll save you!" I yelled. I flung open Gerald's screen door and dashed in.

My feet tangled in the trench coat. I fell facedown in his living room. The horrible sound gradually faded, like a bagpipe running out of air. I scrambled to my feet. I was face-to-face with a surprised-looking woman.

Her hair was even redder than Mae Donna Dockstadter's. It was the color of that stuff Mom sprays my throat with when it is sore. I knew this hair had to be phony; Nature wouldn't play a trick like that on anybody. It was piled into a bun on top of her head. She had what looked like two chopsticks running through the bun. Using my detective expertise, I immediately figured this had to be his aunt. I looked around quickly. "Who was screaming? What happened?" I asked, still panting.

Gerald had this goofy smile plastered across his face, and his eyes looked kind of glazed. He just kept grinning at me without saying anything. Then I saw—he

7

had cotton stuck in his ears. I yanked the cotton out. "What was that noise?" I asked. "Are you in danger?"

Gerald seemed to come to, then. "Noise? Oh, you must mean Aunt Annie. She's rehearsing."

Rehearsing for what? I wondered. Was she doubling as a police siren or something?

She was standing by this little music stand with sheet music lying open on it. She squinted at me through what had to be phony eyelashes—they were too long to be real. "Oh, dear," she said. "I do wish I had my piano here in Scudder instead of back in New York." Four bracelets clanked as she stuck out her hand and smiled at me.

She had long red-lacquered fingernails. I figured they were phony, too. Remembering to be polite, I shook her hand. "Fenton P. Smith," I said. "Do you miss playing your piano?"

She looked at me blankly. "No, dear. I miss my glasses, and that's where I left them—right there on top of the piano next to a cup of cocoa. Oh dear, yes, the cocoa must be pure mold by now. You seem a bit fuzzy without my glasses."

Aunt Annie seemed a bit fuzzy, too, I think.

"The mayor invited her to Scudder," Gerald said proudly. "She's a professional singer—Anastasia Gaborsky—although she's really Annie Grubbs. She's gonna sing and direct an operetta this summer in the new Scudder Civic Theater," he said.

I was relieved to find that Gerald hadn't been tortured or anything. Aunt Annie had just been making soprano noises.

8

"Let's go out on the porch," Gerald said. He still had that silly grin plastered across his face. But he was sniffling. Gerald always does that when he is scared or worried. I figured something was up.

I followed him outside. We slid onto the steps just as his aunt started working on her scales again. *"Aaaaaaaaaaaaaaaooooooooooo."* We'd be lucky if she didn't call every dog in town right here. "What's up?" I asked.

The grin vanished, and a look of pale panic took over. "Fenton, I can't stand much more of this! Scales in the morning. Scales at night. She never stops! Tell me I can come live with you for the summer, please?"

I had this horrible vision of Gerald eating all the food in the house, then starting on the furniture. He's okay for overnight, but for the summer? "Doesn't the cotton in your ears work?" I asked sympathetically.

"It's not just that," Gerald said. "She wants *me* to be in her operetta, Fenton. She thinks it would be 'cute'!"

I cringed. Whenever grown-ups use the word *cute,* it means nothing good for a kid. "Doesn't she know you couldn't carry a tune if you had a bucket in each hand?" I asked. "Once she hears you, she won't—"

Gerald grabbed my arm. "You don't understand! She doesn't care whether I sing or not. She said I could be in the chorus—a walk-on part, she called it."

I patted his hand encouragingly. "Then what's the big deal? If you just walk on, it couldn't be that bad, could it?" I asked.

"Yes it could!" he yelled. "How would *you* like to go

out on a stage in front of strangers and friends wearing a little short skirt—"

"Tunic," I corrected.

"—and carrying a sword?" His eyes were beady and flashed with fear. "Or maybe even a—a Japanese *bathrobe?*"

"Kimono," I soothed. "Doesn't she know she can scar your young mind for life?" I knew I wasn't helping matters, so I tried to be casual. "Well, so you wear a tunic or a kimono. Maybe nobody will even recognize you. And I promise, as your closest friend and fellow detective, I won't tell a soul. Maybe it won't be so bad." Secretly, I was glad it was Gerald and not me.

"No, it's even worse!" he said.

"Worse?" I asked. "What could be worse?"

Gerald wiped some sweat from his forehead, took a deep breath and said, "It's worse because the operetta will be in the Scudder Civic Theater."

"Oh yeah," I said, nodding. "I read about it—sort of—in the paper this morning. It's that old remodeled mansion—Druthers, Drummer—so what's so much worse about that?"

"Drummond," Gerald said. "The worst place to be in the whole world—for any reason. The place is *haunted!*"

Phantom of the Operetta

I stared at my detective partner and best friend. "Haunted? You mean, as in a spook? Ghost? Phantom?"

Gerald sniffled. "Yeah," he said. "Like all of them."

"Oh, wow!" I said. "Our summer is saved! A case to solve. No waiting around for Sticky Fingers Potts to come back to Scudder to rob again. And no more busy-work to keep Mom from thinking I'm a kid headed for trouble. A real case. The phantom of the operetta!"

Gerald looked at me as if I had turned green with pink polka dots. "You have *got* to be kidding. You think we ought to fool around with something that isn't even real?"

"Of course it isn't real," I said. "There's no such thing as ghosts, remember?"

Gerald nodded, gradually understanding. "Oh, yeah. That's right. I forgot. But Aunt Annie said—"

"She's a singer—a stage performer, you know, like an actress. They are always pretending. She probably heard a mouse or something."

12

"But there have been moanings heard," Gerald said. "And people passing by at night have seen lights moving around. And Aunt Annie was sure she saw this awful glowing creature running a—"

"Maybe she is just trying to get some publicity for the operetta—you know, so people will be curious and come, even if they don't want to hear a lot of singing and stuff," I argued.

I leaned back, thinking. "But how can we go undercover to investigate? What clever disguises can we use?"

Gerald shrugged. "Auditions are today. As horrible as being in the operetta would be, it would be a good disguise. Not even Aunt Annie would suspect a thing."

I jumped to my feet and stared at him. "You mean *try out*? You mean volunteer to sing out loud so other people can hear you? You mean volunteer to wear a little skirt—"

"Tunic," Gerald said.

"—and carry a sword, or worse, stand up there in front of everybody and wear a-a-a *bathrobe*?"

"Kimono," Gerald corrected.

Somehow it hadn't seemed nearly as stupid when it was only Gerald. But now . . . I slumped to the step, shoulders sagging. Gerald was right. It was horrible, but it was the best solution available at the moment. And a good detective is willing to look the fool if it gets him the information he needs.

The howling noises inside stopped. Aunt Annie came out on the porch with us. "It's time to have the auditions. Oh, dear," she said. "I do wish I had my garage with me here in Scudder instead of back there in New York."

Following her logic, I asked, "Oh, you miss your car?"

Her cherry-red smile spread across her face. "Oh, no, dear. It's the clothes dryer in the garage that I need. That's where I left my sneakers, and I do need them if I'm going to walk so much here in Scudder."

Gerald rolled his eyes. "Aunt Annie, can Fenton try out at the auditions, too?"

I almost hoped she would say no. But she didn't. "I've posted notices of the tryouts all over Scudder—on telephone poles and the supermarket bulletin boards. It's open to everyone."

I relaxed. Maybe everybody in Scudder had seen the notices. With that many trying out, she probably wouldn't even need us in the operetta at all. We could probably volunteer to paint scenery or something and hang around that way, which was fine with me.

Gerald went home with me so I could shed my disguise. Then we walked the short distance to the Scudder Civic Theater with Aunt Annie. It sure was a spooky-looking building from the outside. It had little turrets and shutters and little round windows that looked like eyes staring at us. The old place looked as if it knew plenty of secrets, but it wasn't telling.

I rubbed my fingers over the big brass numbers nailed to one of the porch pillars. They said 1010. That's 1010 Liberty Street.

Scudder citizens were milling around on the porch, the steps and the lawn. Every size, every shape, they were all there to try out for the operetta. A few of them didn't look as if they were any more anxious for the auditions than I. A couple of kids were whining and tugging at their mothers' hands.

Right in the middle of the crowd, I saw this ketchup-colored head of corkscrew curls. Oh, please, I said to myself, please don't let it be—I sniffed. Lavender!

About that time, the head turned around, and I saw that it was my mortal enemy—Mae Donna Dockstadter. I grabbed Gerald's shoulder and tugged, trying to pull him back behind a crowd of people with me. But it was too late. Dumb old Mae Donna had spotted us. She squirmed through the crowd, her head full of red Slinkies bouncing as she wormed her way toward us.

She glared her little green cat-eyes at me. "What are *you* doing here, Fenton?" she asked. "Don't tell me you are trying to bring a little culture into your dull, dreary life. Or do you actually think that squeaky-door voice of yours will get you a part?"

I narrowed my eyes and glared back. "There are no singing parts for foghorns, Mae Donna. So what are *you* doing here?"

She stuck her chin into the air and looked down her nose at me. "I am further broadening my many talents and expertise to include singing," she said.

Gerald wrinkled his nose. "Broadening my talents and expertise," he mimicked. "Oh, brother!"

"Besides," she said. Her beady little eyes glistened. "Besides, I heard rumors that the place is haunted. Isn't that a *scream*?"

Oh, brother, I thought. She was always butting in on our mysteries. Why couldn't she find something else to do besides wreck our lives?

15

Aunt Annie pulled a big key from her pocket and opened the front door. Everyone fell into something like a herd and followed her inside.

What once was a foyer was now set up with a gilded ticket booth. The dark paneled walls still had pictures, in their carved gold-leaf frames, of Archibald Drummond and Isobel Klein Drummond, the original owners.

We went through the old mahogany doorway and into the auditorium itself. All the room partitions had been knocked out to make one big room with row after row of chairs. It wasn't very big by big-city standards, I guess, but the auditorium was certainly big enough to hold all the Scudder folks who wanted to absorb a bit of culture on any given night.

Glass chandeliers hung from the ceiling, and the walls were covered in a red and silver brocade. The stage with its red velvet curtains took up the far wall. While the others were getting settled, Aunt Annie showed Gerald and me the upstairs rooms, too.

The rest rooms had gold-plated faucets and marble sinks. The dressing rooms for the actors were pastel colors with white wicker folding screens to dress behind and marble-topped dressing tables with rows of lights over the mirrors.

Aunt Annie's dressing table was a mishmash of jars of makeup and tubes of makeup remover and a jewelry case with a lock and even jewelry cleaner all piled and jumbled together as if a hurricane had swept through the room. I smiled to myself, remembering my mom telling me to straighten my room like an adult. This was one adult I could identify with!

16

The prop room had jams of furniture, lamps, pictures, rugs and books everywhere, and the costume storage room—Aunt Annie called it Wardrobe—had racks and racks of dresses and men's clothes from just about any period of history you could imagine. Wow, I thought, if we had access to this place, we'd never want for a disguise again.

After the tour, we followed Aunt Annie back to the auditorium. "Everyone be seated," Aunt Annie said, "and you'll each have a chance to sing for me." To punctuate that, she went through another one of her ear-piercing scales. "*Aaaaaaaaaaaooooooo.*"

"There's good news," Aunt Annie said. "First, the costumes will be furnished for free by the Sam Hill Costume and Party Favors Company. And there will be an extra note of authenticity. The Drummond family jewelry has not been disposed of by the city as yet. Therefore we will be using these *real* jewels in the operetta."

Her hand went to her throat, and she fingered a strand of diamonds. "It will mean publicity and people, and that will mean an audience from the nearby towns, too." She fluttered her eyelashes. "And the other good news is, there're enough parts for *all* of you."

"Nuts!" Gerald said.

"We are performing *The Pirates of Penzance* by Gilbert and Sullivan. I, of course, will sing Mabel." Aunt Annie smiled broadly. "So women and girls who don't sing either Edith, Kate, Isabel or Ruth—the pirate maid-of-all-work—will be the chorus of Major-General Stanley's daughters. And you boys and men who aren't selected as Major-General Stanley; the pirate king;

18

Samuel, his lieutenant; Frederic, the pirate apprentice; or the sergeant of police will sing in the chorus of pirates or police."

I leaned over toward Gerald and whispered. "Maybe it won't be so bad being pirates. *Arrrrr,* mateys. A-vast." At least it wasn't bathrobes or skirts.

One by one, men, women and children went up on the stage. Aunt Annie had the men and boys sing part of the major-general's lines:

I am the very model of a modern Major-General;
I've information vegetable, animal and mineral.

The women and girls sang part of Major-General Stanley's daughters' song:

Go, ye heroes, go to glory,
Though ye die in combat gory,
Ye shall live in song and story.
Go to immortality!

"Gory?" I whispered to Gerald. "Maybe this won't be so bad after all. Maybe it's more exciting than we thought."

"Gory? Ick!" a foghornlike voice whispered. "Oh, yuk!" That had to be dumb old Mae Donna Dock-stadter.

Aunt Annie smiled and nodded, and seemed to be enjoying herself more than anyone—at least more than Gerald and I. I sat there, dreading it as the seats up front emptied out. Soon there were only Mae Donna, Gerald and I left. There wouldn't be any way to get out of this.

It was dumb old Mae Donna's time. She turned to

19

glare at me as if double-daring me to say anything, then pranced up onto the stage as if she owned it. She opened her mouth. I'd heard better sounds when the cat caught her tail in the automatic garage door. She definitely sounded like an authentic police siren.

I was about to give out with a clever remark when suddenly the chandelier overhead made a tinkling sound. I looked up. It was shaking slightly. Then it gradually stopped tinkling, and the one up front shook. Then it, too, stopped. The curtain behind Mae Donna began kind of trembling, as if somebody had hold of it and was shaking it.

Gerald sucked in his breath and let it out with a wheezing suggestion. "The phantom!"

I was not about to be intimidated. I grabbed Gerald's hand and dashed onto the stage, pulling him with me. We passed the surprised Mae Donna, and I jerked back the curtain. I could feel my skin tingle and my hair stand on end.

There was nothing there.

Do You See
What I See?

"Nothing!" I yelled. "There's nothing there! I don't understand." My skin crawled forward over my bones, and my heart thumped hard.

Mae Donna Dockstadter put her hands on her hips and stamped her foot. "You—you creep! You messed up my audition on purpose. Why did you—" Then it must have hit her. Her eyes glinted like little green marbles. "You saw it—didn't you? A ghost. Oh, boy. A real ghost."

"What is going on up there?" Aunt Annie asked. She hopped up on the stage, taking the steps two at a time. "Oh, dear, I do wish I had my apartment right here in Scudder. That's where my aspirin is—right there in the medicine cabinet in my apartment in New York. And I am getting such a headache!"

Since only Gerald, Mae Donna and I were with Aunt Annie, I decided to be honest. "I thought I saw something moving behind the curtain. But when I looked, nobody was there."

21

"I saw it, too," Gerald said. "And the chandelier and
—it was the ghost, the phantom of the operetta."

I tried to be calm and logical the way a good detective would. "Now, we don't know that it was anything
like that," I said, holding my hand up to silence them.
"It could have been a-an earthquake or something."

"Don't be a nerd," Mae Donna said. "We don't have
earthquakes in Scudder."

"All I know is, there is no such thing as ghosts," I
said.

Gerald's voice was shaky. "Then what wears a long
robe and hood and has an awful glowing face?"

"Is this some sort of riddle?" Mae Donna asked.
"It's no time for riddles, Gerald."

"N-n-no," Gerald said. "It's *that!*"

We all looked toward the back of the theater where
Gerald pointed. I could feel my knees give way and
grabbed for the curtain to hold me up. It was true!
There was something horrible, and it dashed for the
exit.

"Run!" I yelled, taking out after it.

I ran to the exit and flung the door open. Whatever
it was, it had vanished. I looked around. "Gerald? Mae
Donna? Aunt Annie?" I called. "Where are you?"

They gradually peered out from behind the curtain
onstage. "You said *run,*" Gerald said. "I thought you
meant *from,* not *after* it."

"I-I was merely looking for a suitable weapon," Mae
Donna said, her nose in the air.

Aunt Annie slumped into one of the audience seats.
"I don't mind ghosts—really I don't. I mean, they were

probably here first, weren't they? So we are really the ones in the way, aren't we? But this one is just downright mean. I just will not put up with a mean ghost, even if he was here first. Do you blame me?"

Any ghost that could stop Mae Donna from singing couldn't be *all* bad. "Not at all," I said. "Just what has this ghost done that is so mean?"

She wiggled one of her red-lacquered fingernails, signaling for us to follow. We did. She led us behind the curtains, among the set backdrops. There was a giant screen with an ocean with a pirate ship on it and one that looked like a burned-out Gothic cathedral. She gave a mighty shove, and the screens rolled away. She pointed to a hole in the wall. "See?" she said. "Everywhere I look, this ghost has knocked holes in the walls. It is so destructive! And people have reported seeing the lights on at night after I have left. And I know I have turned out all the lights. That is, I *think* I have. I just have so much on my mind, you understand."

Gerald sniffled. "Maybe you shouldn't have an operetta," he said. His voice seemed full of hope. I could understand his feelings about parading around onstage in front of everybody. Still, I wanted to solve this mystery. And we couldn't do it if Aunt Annie chickened out and closed down.

Aunt Annie pulled one of the chopsticks from her bun and stuck it in at another angle. "No," she said. "I came here to give Scudder a touch of culture, and that's what I'm going to do. You children be here for rehearsals starting tomorrow. I'll post the cast assignments this afternoon." She smiled. "I just know you dear children will love being in the chorus."

23

While I didn't relish being in Aunt Annie's operetta, at least it gave me a chance to hang around and solve this thing for her.

Aunt Annie told us she was going to shop a bit in downtown Scudder. Gerald and I watched her lock the door, then we walked all around the outside, checking to see that all the windows and exits were locked. I motioned for Gerald to follow me. We had some deduction to do. We looked all around. Good. Dumb old Mae Donna wasn't in sight. We walked back to Gerald's house, taking a roundabout route in case Mae Donna had any plans for following us. We sure didn't want her getting in the way of our sleuthing.

Gerald got us a couple of soft drinks, and we sat in the porch swing. It squeaked as we eased it back and forth and talked. "Okay," I said, "first thing is, we don't believe in ghosts."

"We don't?" Gerald asked. "Are you sure we don't?"

"Positive," I said. "It's all an invention of the late-night moviemakers. That means it is a living, breathing person that is haunting the theater. As good detectives, we must look for motive and opportunity."

Gerald sipped his drink and swallowed. "Agreed," he said. "But what motive does this ghost—this living, breathing person—have?"

"What about greed?" a new voice asked. "That's always a good guess."

I sniffed. Lavender perfume attacked my nose. "Mae Donna Dockstadter! Why are you spying on us? This is *our* case," I yelled.

The bushes rustled as she came out from behind them. "What took you guys so long to get here? I've been waiting over twenty minutes!" Her kinky corkscrew curls bounced as she bounded up the steps and plopped herself onto the swing right between Gerald and me.

"Well, *join* us, Mae Donna," I growled.

"Thanks," she replied as if she didn't know I was being sarcastic. "I can see you two nerds need help on this. And I, Mae Donna Dockstadter, daughter of the famous secret agent, will come to your rescue."

Gerald rolled his eyes. "Oh, brother! How did we get so *lucky?*"

Ignoring us, Mae Donna continued. "Now, here's what I think. I think that the theater is worth more to somebody empty than with operettas and plays and stuff going on."

That seemed logical, but I wasn't going to let Mae Donna know I hadn't thought that far through the case. "Obviously, Mae Donna," I said. "But the real problem is in figuring out just why—and who."

I suddenly remembered the article by Samantha Twill, the town historian, I had seen in the Scudder newspaper. "Gerald, do you have today's newspaper?" I asked. "There's an article in there about the theater."

Gerald got the newspaper, and the three of us huddled over the article, reading.

"It says the mansion was built by the Drummonds, and they left it to the city when the last Drummond died," Gerald said. His eyes widened. "Do you think the ghost is one of the Drummonds?" He withered under my glare. "Oh, yeah. I forgot. We don't believe in ghosts."

I read further. "Ummm, the will said if the city didn't use the property in behalf of the whole community by this year, it could be sold off and the money donated to charity. That lets out the greed motive—you know, like when some heir wants his grubby hands on it. But maybe somebody wants to buy it for themselves and build one of those big high-rise offices or hotels on the property or something that would bring in lots of money. Maybe they figure on discouraging the city from using the property."

Mae Donna nodded smugly. "See? Greed! Didn't I tell you?"

"Maybe it's the mayor," Gerald said.

"The mayor!" I said.

"Yeah, look what he said in the article," Gerald argued. "The land would be worth more to the city as business property because it would bring in taxes. Maybe he doesn't *want* the theater to be successful. Maybe he wants it to be auctioned off so the city can have more tax money."

"Dumb," I said. "There's no way the mayor could benefit from taxes—not personally, anyway. But look here! There's a statement by the Scudder Heritage Society president, Samantha Twill. She is really hot under the collar about the renovation. She thought the mansion ought to be preserved just as it was for a museum. Do you think she is doing all the damage to run Aunt Annie and the others off?"

"Sure," Mae Donna said. "A ninety-year-old lady is

27

sneaking around in the dark and knocking holes in the walls. Don't be *weird,* Fenton!"

I narrowed my eyes at her. If it weren't for her father, I'd—her father! That's it. "I think it is time to ask Mr. Dockstadter's advice," I said.

Mae Donna's face went beet red—about the same as her hair. Her freckles vanished in a sea of red. "Oh, no!" she said. "Don't even *say* that." The red gradually faded into a pasty gray. "He—he's undercover. You don't want to blow his cover, do you?"

I grinned. It was fun to see Mae Donna squirm, for a change. And if it helped solve the crime, too, what could be better?

Some Good Advice

There was no way Mae Donna Dockstadter was going to keep me from consulting her father. She huffed and puffed and snapped and snarled all the way.

When we got to the Dockstadter house, I spotted Mr. Dockstadter on top of his undercover van—Dockstadter Exterminator/No Stone Unchecked. He was on top of his van bolting down a giant plastic bug with wiry antennae.

"Wouldn't people feel more confident if the bug were feet up, as if he were dead, Mr. Dockstadter?" I asked.

Mr. Dockstadter looked up. "Why, Finkly—"

"Fenton, sir."

"And Gaston—"

"Gerald!"

"Hello," he said. "You know, Farron, I believe you are right! Why didn't I think of that?"

I blushed appropriately. "Why, sir, you have so many more important things on your mind like—"

"Fenton!" Mae Donna interrupted. "Let's go!"

I glared at her and continued. "Like getting all those undesirables off the street."

Mr. Dockstadter smiled so that his freckles melted into one, just like Mae Donna's did. "Hmmm, out of our houses and buildings, Farley. I leave the streets to the city boys."

I nodded. "I understand, sir. Departmental jealousies." I wasn't too sure what that meant, but I had heard Dad complain about it a couple of times, and it sounded impressive.

"Why, Falder, it isn't often that I find one so young so understanding about my business."

"Oh, heck, sir," I said, blushing an even deeper red. "You probably don't remember—since you have so many things on your mind—but I, and Gerald here, too, are going to be just like you when we grow up." Frankly, I thought I'd find a more dignified cover than a bug man, though I wouldn't knock his using it.

"Wonderful," he said. "Just wonderful. Someday we'll win this war on vermin."

I cleared my throat—this was getting too emotional for him. "Speaking of vermin, sir, I need some advice."

"Fenton P. Smith, come on!" Mae Donna pleaded.

"We believe we have an 'undesirable' in the Scudder Civic Theater—you know, the old Drummond mansion," I said. "Do you have any suggestions?"

"I could die," Mae Donna said. "I could just *die!*"

Mr. Dockstadter leaned against his van and stared off into the distance as if he were seeing something none of us could see. "Farrington, these old buildings are a

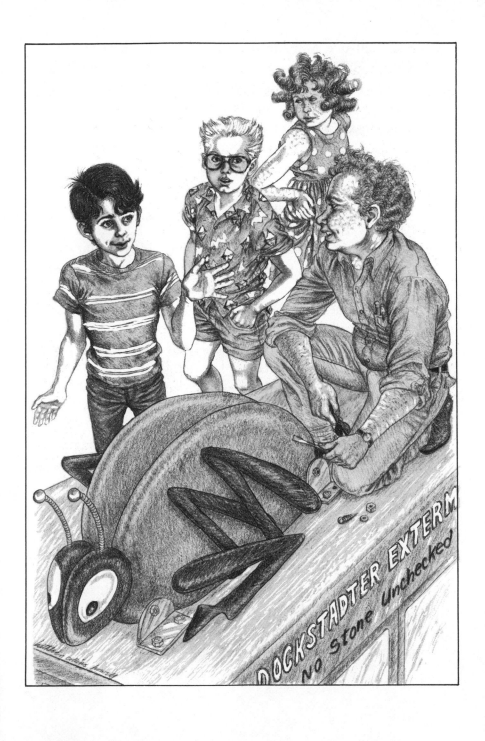

real challenge. Some of them have passages between the walls and between the ceilings and floors wide enough to crawl through, and huge attics and basements and even sub-basements. That's where I'd look for the vermin. Yessir, a real challenge."

"Gee, thanks, Mr. Dockstadter," I said, offering him my hand. We shook hands. "Thanks loads. You've been a big help."

He saluted. "Anything to help out the next generation of vermin busters."

He talked kind of weird, sometimes. Maybe that was in code. But it made sense. Whoever this phantom was, he could be hiding in any one of those places Mr. Dockstadter suggested. "We've got our work cut out for us —you, too, Mae Donna. You can help." I figured we'd need all the help we could get. I felt I owed it to Mr. Dockstadter to be nice to his daughter. For a little while, anyway. Besides, dark passages were just the place for a creep like Mae Donna Dockstadter.

"Oh, geeeeeee, thanks," Mae Donna said. "How could I ever thank you enough? Oh, geeee." She stuck her nose in the air. "Thanks, but no thanks, Fenton P. Smith. You just figure it out on your own—if you think you can. And I bet you that I solve the mystery of the phantom of the operetta before you two nerds do. So there!"

Boy! Try to do somebody a favor and what does it get you? Abuse and double-daring, that's what. I stood there with my hands in my pocket, watching Mae Donna stalk off down the sidewalk. Her red curls bounced on her head like a Slinky marathon.

"Gerald," I said, "we not only have got to solve this case, but we have got to solve it fast—before that dumb old Mae Donna Dockstadter does."

"Maybe with the two of you working on it, I'd just be in the way," Gerald said. He sniffled.

"Are you forgetting again that there is no such thing as ghosts, Gerald?" I asked.

"Yeah, sort of," he said, sniffling again. "But it is hard to remember there are no such things as ghosts when one rattles the chandeliers and rumples the curtains, Fenton."

"I have an idea about that," I said. "But first we have got to find some disguises that will get us into the theater but out from under Aunt Annie's eye. I've got it! We'll dress up like city janitors. No, she'd expect us to be cleaning up, and we wouldn't have time to snoop."

"What about city inspectors?" Gerald asked.

"Gerald, you're a genius!" I said. It wasn't often I could compliment my junior partner, so I did whenever I could. "Get in disguise and meet me in front of the theater in twenty minutes," I instructed.

I rushed home and rummaged through my closet. I found an old suit of my dad's, the felt hat I'd used at the newspaper office, and a handlebar moustache. I got a yardstick and a notebook and pencil.

When I got to the theater, Gerald was waiting. He had on a derby, a nose that was big enough to belong to Cyrano, and a sport jacket that looked as if it had been made from a horse blanket.

We went inside. Aunt Annie was there, pacing back and forth. Gerald kept his head down so she couldn't

33

see his face. I touched the tip of my hat and nodded. "City inspector here," I said, lowering my voice. "We've come to check the wiring and—and stuff."

"Oh, dear, I was hoping you were the sheriff. Press," she said. "If you are an inspector, how come your hat says *Press*?"

Rats! I had forgotten to take out the press card. I cleared my throat. "Errrrhem, that's a note to the cleaners," I said. "Press."

Aunt Annie shrugged. "I'd still rather you be the sheriff. I did call him, I think. Yes, I'm sure of it. I called him."

"And why do you need the sheriff, ma'am?" I asked.

Aunt Annie clutched her throat. "Why, the Drummond jewels have been stolen. From right around my neck! No, no, I take that back. I took them off. I put them to soak in the jewelry cleaner and locked them in the safe this morning. But when I went to get them this afternoon, they weren't there. The phantom took them. But that is no concern of yours, of course. The sheriff will handle that. You do know that there is already a city inspector here."

"There is?" I asked, my voice breaking into a shriek. I lowered it. "I mean, there is?" Then it hit me. "Would she have hair the color of a raw hot dog? And it sort of springs all over her head?"

Aunt Annie nodded. "Yes, that's the one. Short, with red hair and big glasses and orthopedic shoes."

"Errrrhem," I said. "Good to know my *assistant* is on the job. Have to watch her every second, you know."

Aunt Annie waved her hand. "So inspect," she said.

"I have work to do." She punctuated that with a loud *"la la la la la la lah!"*

"C'mon, Gerald," I whispered. I felt a surge of excitement. We not only had to solve the mystery of the phantom, but we had to find the stolen jewels. What more could a Determined Detective want in life than two mysteries at once!

Close Encounters
of the Worst Kind

Gerald and I walked around, poking at light switches and tapping walls. When Aunt Annie was convinced we were busy, she went backstage to wait for the sheriff.

"You know what worries me?" Gerald whispered as he tapped a wall. "What if we find the phantom? Then what?"

"Gerald," I said, "you keep forgetting that the phantom is really a person. When we find the phantom, we simply detain him until the police arrive."

"Good," Gerald said. "You detain him. I'll go call the police."

I don't know how I got saddled with a partner like Gerald. If only he were as brave as I am. Besides, we should take turns detaining. It was my turn to go for help.

I tapped the wall. Once, twice, three times. The wall tapped back. I tapped again. The wall tapped again. Slowly I tapped, working my way toward the door. The taps seemed to follow me. I gave one last tap and leaped through the door. I came face-to-face with Mae Donna Dockstadter.

"Go home!" I growled.

"You go home!" she growled back.

"Okay," I said. "We might as well split up and search. We can cover more space that way, maybe locate the jewels, even if we don't find the phantom. Mae Donna, you take the attic. I'll take the cellar. Gerald, you—"

"I'm going with you," he said. Gerald sniffled. His eyes were wide and staring.

Mae Donna narrowed her little green eyes at me and crossed her arms defensively. "I'll take the cellar," she said. "You take the attic."

"Fine!" I yelled. "Take something. And I'll go in the opposite direction." That was exactly where I wanted to be. In the opposite direction from Mae Donna Dockstadter.

Mae Donna went off down the hall to locate the door to the cellar. I, with Gerald following close behind, started up the stairs. We went past the second floor, where the rest rooms and storage rooms were, and up a flight of narrower stairs to a door. I opened it slowly, quietly.

I heard the rustle of paper and sound of steps on the other side. "Mice!" I said, as much to convince myself as Gerald.

"Big mice with big feet!" Gerald whispered as I flung open the door.

We stood staring at not one but two weird-looking guys. My heart nearly stopped, and I flung my hand up protectively. The guy opposite me flung his hand up, too.

I let out a big wheezing breath. It was a mirror, and the two not-at-all–weird-looking guys were Gerald and me. My relief was brief, however. In the shadows, something moved. Gerald's fingers dug into my arm.

I squinted toward the shadows, trying to make out what was there. It was big, and it seemed to be draped in some sort of dark cloak. Suddenly the face turned toward us, and it glowed. It actually glowed! The cloak hood slowly slid back to reveal big greenish ears like bat wings.

Gerald and I each sucked in our breaths at the same time. We stood there, clinging to each other, staring. The cloaked figure shoved some boxes toward us, and we dodged. There was suddenly a musty smell in the air, and the thing we'd been staring at was no longer there. It had vanished right before our eyes!

"T-t-t-tell me one more t-t-t-time," Gerald said. "T-t-t-tell me there's no s-s-s-such thing as g-g-ghosts."

I blinked, trying to clear my eyes. I hadn't seen what I saw. I knew that. So how come I thought I saw what I hadn't seen?

I took a deep breath and looked around the attic. Then I saw something that made me feel a lot better. "Look," I told Gerald, pointing to a stack of boxes. On top was a jar of peanut butter and a half loaf of bread. And there were some empty juice cans, too. "Ghosts don't eat, Gerald," I said. "That is, if there were such things as ghosts, they wouldn't eat." He was even confusing me now.

"Are you sure?" Gerald said.

"Look," I said. "There is even a copy of the Scudder newspaper, the one with the article on the theater."

"But it glowed," Gerald insisted. "I saw it, and it glowed. Then it disappeared."

"Did somebody here lose a ghost?" a foghorn voice behind us asked.

I swallowed my fright and managed to say, "A fairly good imitation of one, anyway." I was not about to let Mae Donna know that the whole thing had shaken me up almost as badly as it had Gerald.

"Well, I think I found it—at least for a minute," Mae Donna said. "I was snooping around the basement when suddenly it was there. Then it wasn't. It was in some sort of cloak, and its face and horrible ears glowed."

"Up here in the attic? Down there in the basement?" Gerald said. "Maybe we are dealing with *two* ghosts! I mean, if there were such a thing, that is."

"Ghosts don't eat, and they don't read newspapers," I said. "If we search well enough, we will no doubt find the trapdoors that open into the crawl spaces and some sort of hidden staircase down to the cellar. That *has* to be why we smell the musty odor when the ghost appears or disappears. All that air trapped in the crawl spaces gets stale and dusty."

At least, I hoped that was the reason. I had to sound hearty for Gerald's sake. "Don't worry. What we are dealing with is a human being who is trying to scare everyone away."

"Well, he—or she—is doing a pretty good job of that," Gerald said. "I am ready to give it up."

"Mr. Dockstadter was right," I said. "He told us to look in the basement and in the cellar and the crawl spaces."

"Will you cut it out about what my father says?" Mae Donna said. "Let's just get on with this case, okay?"

"Whoever this guy is, he already knows a lot of the secret places. And there aren't enough of us to be at every possible exit. So we are just going to have to figure out a way to smoke him out."

Gerald gasped. "You mean set fire to the place?"

"Naw," I said. "We have got to figure out why he is here and lure him out."

"It'd help if we knew who it was," Mae Donna said.

"We'd know who it was if we could catch him," Gerald said.

"And we could catch him and find out who he is if we only knew what he wanted," I said.

I sighed. It seemed we had a lot of questions. But no answers at all.

Ta Da Dump!

I picked up the newspaper, hoping that I'd find the diamonds there on the box along with the peanut butter and bread. That's when I noticed that the phantom had really worked the newspaper over.

There was a red circle around the story about the theater, which seemed natural enough since this is where he was. But it was what was *not* there that really caught my attention. There was a neat cutout where the story about Sticky Fingers had been.

This guy was interested enough in Sticky Fingers to not just circle the article but to cut it out and save it. Why?

I remembered the clippings I had copied at the newspaper office, the ones written fifteen years ago about Perciphal "Sticky Fingers" Potts. I pulled them from my pocket. Gerald leaned over my right shoulder, reading along.

The stench of lavender perfume nearly knocked me over, as Mae Donna Dockstadter leaned over my left shoulder to read. "Pa-leeeze," I yelled. "I'll read aloud.

42

It says here that Sticky Fingers was arrested at his home, 1010 Liberty, in his room. That must be a typographical error. This is 1010 Liberty."

"The Drummond mansion became a boarding house in 1965," Mae Donna said.

I glared at her.

"It says so right in the article on the theater," Mae Donna said, glaring back. "That's five years before Sticky Fingers was arrested."

I made a mental note to read all the way through articles from now on, even if they are dull. You never know when information might come in handy. "He could have been boarding here," I said. I remembered how the ghost's ears seemed to protrude. I looked again at my clipping of Sticky Fingers. "At least we all know who the ghost is."

"No we don't," Gerald said. "At least, not all of us."

"Come on, Gerald," I coaxed. It was embarrassing the way my junior partner could overlook the obvious sometimes. "Sticky Fingers, right? Living right here when he was arrested, right? Money never found, okay? Got it?"

"Ohhh," Gerald said. "You think Sticky Fingers is the ghost. You think he hid the money here, huh."

"Right!" Mae Donna and I said at the same time. Sometimes Gerald really worries me.

"He is just wandering around the different cubbyholes looking. That's why he wanted everybody out of here. So he could look without being seen. He doesn't recognize anything after the alterations. He doesn't know where his money is."

"I do," Gerald said.

"Huh?" Mae Donna and I said at the same time again. I shuddered, worrying that we were beginning to think alike.

"How do you know!" I demanded. How *could* Gerald know when I, Fenton P. Smith, founder and senior detective of the Determined Detectives, didn't know?

"I read the *whole* article on the Drummond mansion," Gerald said. "It said that all the walls that were pulled from the mansion were carried out to the dump. He probably hid it in his room, don't you think?"

"Of course I think!" I said. If Gerald had figured this out, surely Sticky Fingers had figured it out, too. "We had better get to the dump quick. One of you stay here and tell the sheriff when he comes to investigate the diamond theft, then meet us at the dump."

"Wait a minute, buster," Mae Donna snarled. "What do you mean *one of us* stay and call the sheriff while *you* go to the dump? Why can't you stay here and . . ."

"We're wasting time," I said, "valuable time. I'll stay here because it is more important to tell the sheriff anyway."

Mae Donna narrowed her eyes at me. "I'll stay and tell the sheriff. You two get out to the dump. And don't lose him! I'll catch up to you."

I grinned as I ran. It had worked. Dumb old Mae Donna was staying here—out of my way. With any luck, it would all be over by the time she got to the dump.

Gerald and I started running—it isn't very far to anything in Scudder. If we ran, it shouldn't take more than ten minutes to get there. As I ran, this dumb old song kept ringing in my head, the one to the tune of the *William Tell* Overture—*ta da dump, ta da dump, ta da dump dump dump!*

Gerald and I sprinted for the street. We skirted around people who lazily strolled along the sidewalks. My heart pounded. My moustache was hanging by only one hair, and my *Press* sign had fallen from my brown felt hat.

At the entrance to the dump, I stopped, panting. Gerald caught up to me, and we looked around. A few people were scrounging around the dump, pulling out old broken lamps and bent golf clubs and junk like that. I spotted this one guy on his hands and knees rummaging around big piles of lumber. His ears stuck out something fierce. "Over there!" I said.

About that time, I was knocked to my knees—*ooph*.

"Sorry," Mae Donna said. "I used my skateboard to catch up. I keep it in my bag—just in case."

"Just great," I moaned. "I'd really *hate* for you to miss the good stuff. Is the sheriff on his way?"

Her green eyes sort of bugged out. "The sheriff! Oh my gosh. I forgot to see. I just told him and ran."

"Look!" I said. "He's got something in his hand— a laundry bag. I'll bet it contains the money that he stole and hid away all these years. He's getting up. He'll get away!"

I suddenly had an idea. I spotted a piece of paper fluttering and rolled it up like a megaphone. "Mae Donna," I whispered. "Hide here behind this box. And sing—you know, like you did at the auditions."

45

She blinked her green cat-eyes at me. "Sing? You want me to sing *now*?"

"Yes," I hissed. "Gerald, you get over there. And don't say anything except 'Right, Chief.' "

He sniffled. "If you say so," he said.

That's what I like about Gerald. He figures I've got something good up my sleeve and doesn't ask questions —not like that dumb old Mae Donna.

From my crouched position behind an old discarded chest of drawers, I said, "*Psssst,* sing!"

Mae Donna opened her big mouth and sang— "*Arrrrraooooooooo. Arrrrrroooooooah!*"

Just as I figured. It sounded exactly like a police siren. Old Sticky Fingers must have thought so, too. He looked up, pale white. His ears sort of flapped as he swallowed hard.

I signaled Mae Donna to shut up. Then I yelled through the rolled-up paper, "Stop where you are, Sticky Fingers! You are surrounded. Right, men?"

Right on signal, Gerald said, "Right, Chief."

From Mae Donna's post came another "Right, Chief." I guess I couldn't argue with her padding her part. It did seem more impressive to have three voices instead of two.

Where were the sheriff and his men? They should have been here by now. What if he didn't believe Mae Donna? I yelled into the paper. "Drop the money, Sticky Fingers. And put your hands behind your head. Lie facedown on the ground. And shut your eyes. Don't even look up."

He dropped the money and did as I told him. Mae

46

Donna had spotted a piece of pipe on the ground. She ran over and stuck it to his back as if it were the barrel of a gun. "Don't peek!" she snarled in her foghorn voice.

Gerald and I used our belts to tie his hands and feet. At last, the sheriff drove up, and we handed over Sticky Fingers and the money to him.

"Before you take him away, Sheriff," I said, "I'd like to ask him one question. What did you do with the jewelry you stole from Aunt Annie?"

"I didn't take no jewelry. I just took my money. And you can't take me nowhere. I done served my time on the money."

"I think we can come up with some new charges, Sticky Fingers. You weren't given a key to the theater, so how about breaking and entering for a start?" the sheriff said. "And those holes in the walls are willful destruction of property. And we'll think of a few other things to hold you awhile, too."

"And impersonating a ghost," Gerald added.

Just in case some of the finer details of the case had escaped Gerald and Mae Donna's logic, I quickly filled them in. "The old Drummond mansion is riddled with secret passages," I reminded them. "And when old Sticky Fingers would crawl through the one between the first-floor ceiling and the floor above, it would make the chandeliers shake, remember?"

Mae Donna stuck her nose into the air. "We're not *dense*, Fenton. That's why the shaking chandeliers started at the back of the theater then gradually worked their way up front where the curtain started to shake a little." She crossed her arms, self-satisfied.

This was *my* moment, so I quickly took over again. "Then he got on and off the stage through one of those holes he'd knocked in the wall behind the big pieces of scenery. Nothing spooky about that!" I said.

Gerald didn't look too convinced. "But what about his face? That glowed. And that's pretty spooky."

I opened my mouth to explain, but dumb old Mae Donna cut in. "Theatrical makeup," she said. "He just smeared it on his face, and when the lights were low, the makeup picked up enough of the small amount of light to reflect it. You can even get that junk at Halloween. No big mystery." She screwed up her face, her green cat-eyes wide. "But there's still something that bothers me. If Sticky Fingers didn't take the jewelry, who did?"

I suddenly grinned. It all fell into place. "Come on back to the theater," I said. "Inspector Smith will meet you in the dressing room, where he will uncover the missing jewelry." I crossed my fingers that I was right.

As Smooth as Cream

Aunt Annie was at the theater when we got back. She followed us into her dressing room.

"Sticky Fingers Potts says he did not steal the diamonds," I said, pacing back and forth and scratching my chin thoughtfully. "While he is not the most honest man in the world, I believe him. I remembered Aunt Annie's, er, ah, *logic*—you know, wanting her garage so she could have her sneakers, which were on the dryer in the garage at her apartment in New York—that sort of thing. And I thought maybe I could follow her brand of logic and find the jewels."

"And did you?" she asked.

I saw that I had the others' attention, too, and just hoped that I was right. Fenton P. Smith does not like to look the fool.

"Aunt Annie sometimes gets, er"—I struggled to find a nice way of putting it—"er, distracted. So I thought, what would an actress do when she has been wearing real jewelry? She would put it away. But first, she would clean it of any makeup. So—"

50

I reached for the jar of jewelry cleaner that was on her dressing table. I could feel my heart sink. It was gone. I cleared my throat and continued pacing. "So I am sure that was her intention. But that is not the case, as you will see." Come on, Fenton P. Smith, get with it, I told myself.

"I already told you I soaked the jewels in the cleaner," Aunt Annie said impatiently. "And I locked them in the safe, see?" She quickly spun the dial on the wall safe and opened it. Sure enough, there was the jar of cleaner.

"May I see that?" I asked.

"Certainly, dear," Aunt Annie said. "But it's empty."

I panicked. What if I couldn't produce the jewels? What if I was wrong? "Er, first, maybe you would like to ask questions about the phantom case. I wouldn't want to leave any of you in the dark on that one. Like for instance, Sticky Fingers felt if he could scare everyone away from the theater with this ghost gimmick he could have more time to search for his money. It wasn't until today—when the Scudder newspaper did the story —that he realized his wall was not even here anymore, that . . ."

"Cut it out, Fenton," Mae Donna said. "Do you know where the jewels are or not?"

I raised an eyebrow and glared at her. "I'm coming to that. A good detective must set the mood, must . . ." I paced some more, looking for inspiration to strike. My eyes lit on the dressing table with all the jars of makeup, the brushes and the jar of cold cream. . . . Inspiration struck!

I cleared my throat and wrapped the fingers of my left hand around the lapel of my jacket and twirled the ends of my false moustache with my right. "Aunt Annie said everybody looked fuzzy without her glasses, if you will remember. So wouldn't every*thing* look fuzzy, too? She came into the dressing room, removed the jewels and dumped them in the jar of cleaner to soak.

"Then she was distracted by something—the phantom, perhaps—and when she picked up the jar to lock it in the safe, she only *thought* she had the same jar. . . ." I opened the jar of cold cream and triumphantly pulled out a handful of jewelry in a mess of icky white glop.

"So," I said as modestly as any superb detective could, "case closed."

Aunt Annie squealed and hugged me hard.

The sheriff shook my hand.

Mae Donna shrugged. "Whatever," she said.

"And, boys," Aunt Annie said, "now that our ghost is out of the way, we can get on with the operetta." She patted our cheeks as if we were chubby babies. "You have the cutest little costumes."

Gerald and I both groaned. There was that word again—*cute!* I'd rather face Sticky Fingers again than *cute.*